Scion™

BLOOD FOR BLOOD

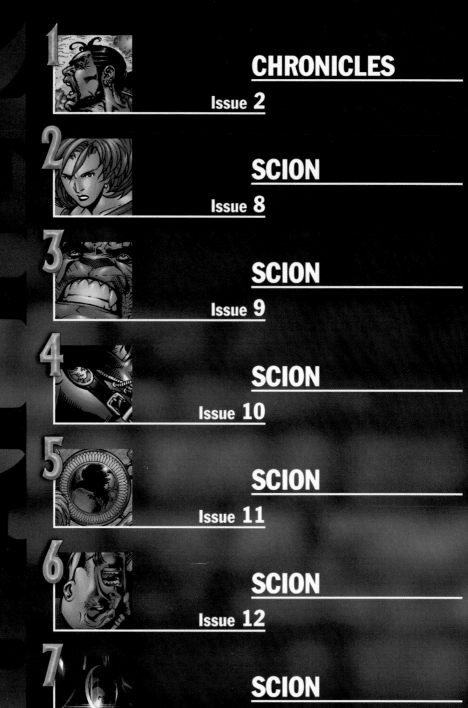
Scion™: **Blood For Blood** Vol. 2, MARCH 2002. FIRST PRINTING. Originally published in single magazine form as **Scion**™ Vol. 1, Issues #8-#14, and **CrossGen Chronicles**™ Vol. 1, Issue #2. Copyright © 2000, 2001, 2002. All rights reserved. Published by CrossGeneration Comics, Inc. Office of publication: 4023 Tampa Road, Suite 2400, Oldsmar, Florida 34677. **CrossGen**®, **CrossGen Comics**®, **CrossGeneration**® and **CrossGeneration Comics**® are registered trademarks of CrossGeneration Comics, Inc. **Scion**™, the **CrossGen sigil**™, **CrossGen Chronicles**™ and all prominent characters are ™ and © 2002 CrossGeneration Comics, Inc. All rights reserved. The entire contents of this book are ™ and © 2002 CrossGeneration Comics, Inc. The stories, incidents and characters in this publication are fictional. Any similarities to persons living or dead are purely coincidental. With the exception of artwork used for review purposes, none of the contents of this book may be reproduced in any form without the express written consent of CrossGeneration Comics, Inc. PRINTED IN CANADA.

Avalon is actually two worlds: one, a medieval façade that maintains a connection with the planet's feudal past; the other, the fabulous technology hidden beneath that veneer. Science has enabled the creation of everything from hovercraft that skim the sea's surface, to the diversity of life-forms known as the Lesser Races that were spawned through genetic manipulation.

ETHAN

SKINK

BERND

Two great dynasties, the Herons of the West and the Ravens of the East, have ruled Avalon for centuries. Their long-standing hatreds run deep and the kingdoms warred for centuries until a fragile truce was forged. That truce was shattered by a young Heron prince named Ethan. After being branded with a sigil whose power he could neither understand nor control, Ethan scarred the Raven heir to the throne, Bron, during the annual tournament of ritual combat that had replaced open warfare.

KING VIKTOR

ASHLEIGH

BRON

Ethan surrendered himself to the Ravens, but was soon freed from his imprisonment by a woman named Ashleigh, who wanted Ethan to join the Underground's cause of freedom for the Lesser Races. Ethan declined her offer and returned home as the clouds of war gathered on the horizon.

The initial battle was met upon the Western shore at Point Korday, Ethan fighting at the side of his brothers, Kai and Artor, and sister, Ylena. Ultimate victory belonged to the Herons, but at a terrible price. Artor, heir to the throne, was brutally slain by Bron. As Artor was laid to rest in the family crypt, a man calling himself Bernd Rechts appeared and offered his services as war advisor. Rechts showed great interest in Ethan's sigil, but could not dissuade the young prince from departing for the East so he could avenge his brother's death.

HE PUSHED THE HERONS AND RAVENS TOWARD PEACE MORE THAN A CENTURY AGO. AND NOW WE'RE AT WAR AGAIN...

WHOKT

...BECAUSE OF *ME.*

ETHAN, SOMETIMES YOUR DESTINY CHOOSES *YOU,* RATHER THAN YOU CHOOSING IT. DON'T BLAME YOURSELF FOR THINGS BEYOND YOUR CONTROL.

LIKE THE WAR?

LIKE MY BROTHER'S MURDER?

THERE'S NO NEED TO SPARE MY FEELINGS, SKINK. WE'VE KNOWN EACH OTHER TOO LONG.

THE TRUTH IS NONE OF THIS WOULD'VE HAPPENED IF *I* HADN'T CAUSED IT...

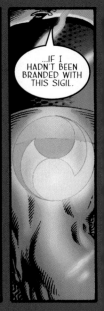

...IF I HADN'T BEEN BRANDED WITH THIS SIGIL.

MOST PEOPLE *CELEBRATE* ON THEIR BIRTHDAYS.

I SET TWO KINGDOMS TO WAR.

THEY FORGED ME THE SWORD OF THE MAN WHO BROUGHT THE HERON-RAVEN WAR TO AN END.

AND I HAVE EVERY INTENTION OF USING IT TO *KILL* A RAVEN PRINCE.

NO ONE WOULD ARGUE YOUR VOW TO AVENGE ARTOR'S DEATH, ETHAN. IT'S A MATTER OF HONOR.

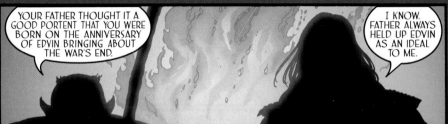

YOUR FATHER THOUGHT IT A GOOD PORTENT THAT YOU WERE BORN ON THE ANNIVERSARY OF EDVIN BRINGING ABOUT THE WAR'S END.

I KNOW. FATHER ALWAYS HELD UP EDVIN AS AN IDEAL TO ME.

BUT I DON'T THINK I'VE DONE A VERY GOOD JOB OF LIVING UP TO HIS LEGACY.

EDVIN WAS ADMIRAL OF THE HERON FLEET...

...LOYAL BROTHER TO THE KING...

...THE *PEACE MAKER*...

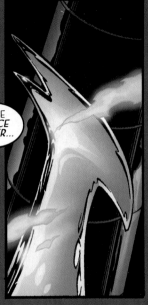

...HOW AM I SUPPOSED TO FIND A RAVEN FLEET THAT SEEMS DETERMINED TO HIDE FROM US?

I'VE NO TASTE FOR THIS CAT AND MOUSE GAME, GRUM. I BEGIN TO WONDER IF WE'RE THE HUNTER OR THE HUNTED.

SIRE, DISPATCHES HAVE ARRIVED.

THE WEATHER'S BLOWING IN FROM THE NORTH AND IS EXPECTED TO WORSEN.

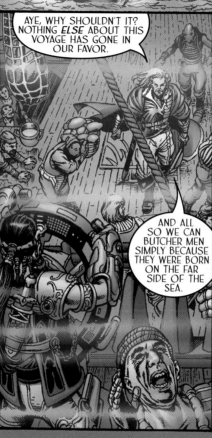

AYE, WHY SHOULDN'T IT? NOTHING ELSE ABOUT THIS VOYAGE HAS GONE IN OUR FAVOR.

AND ALL SO WE CAN BUTCHER MEN SIMPLY BECAUSE THEY WERE BORN ON THE FAR SIDE OF THE SEA.

WE HERONS AND RAVENS HAVE BEEN AT EACH OTHER'S THROATS FOR SO LONG WE DON'T EVEN REMEMBER WHY WE FIGHT. FOOLS, ALL OF US, FOOLS.

BUT IT'S NOT MY PLACE TO GAINSAY MY KINGDOM OR MY KING, EVEN WHEN IT'S MY BROTHER WHO SITS ON THE THRONE.

ADMIRAL EDVIN!

SIGHTING TO PORT!

FINALLY.

GLASS!

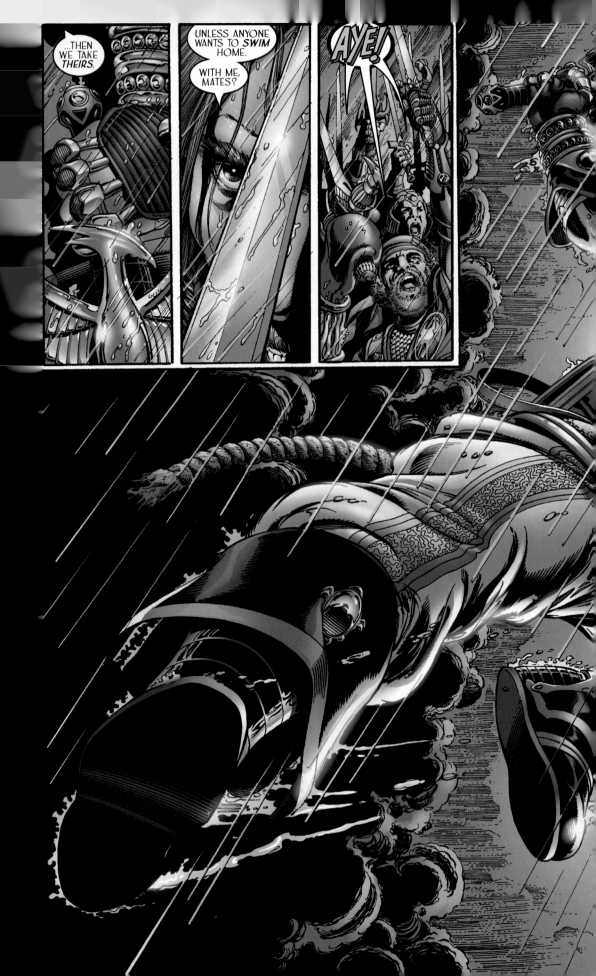

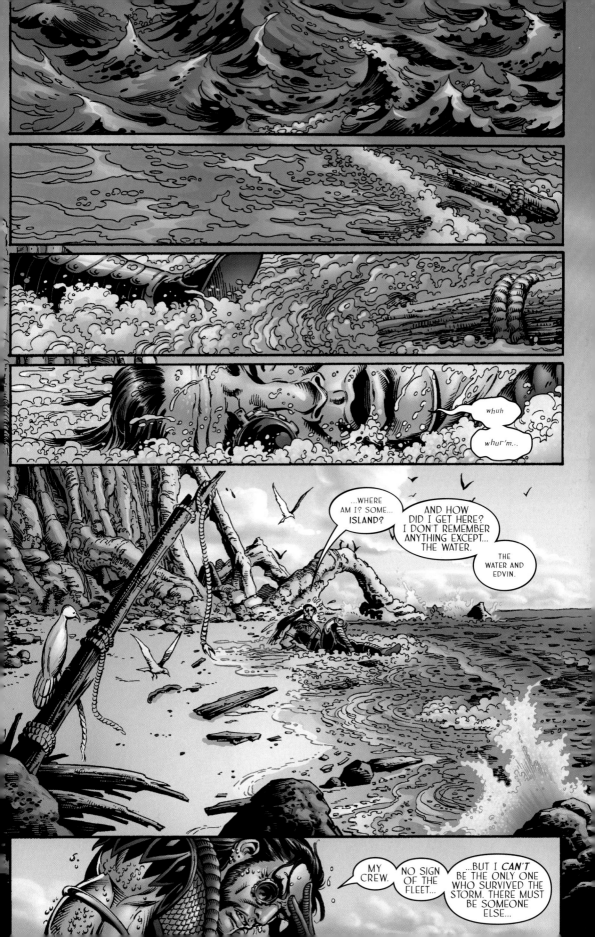

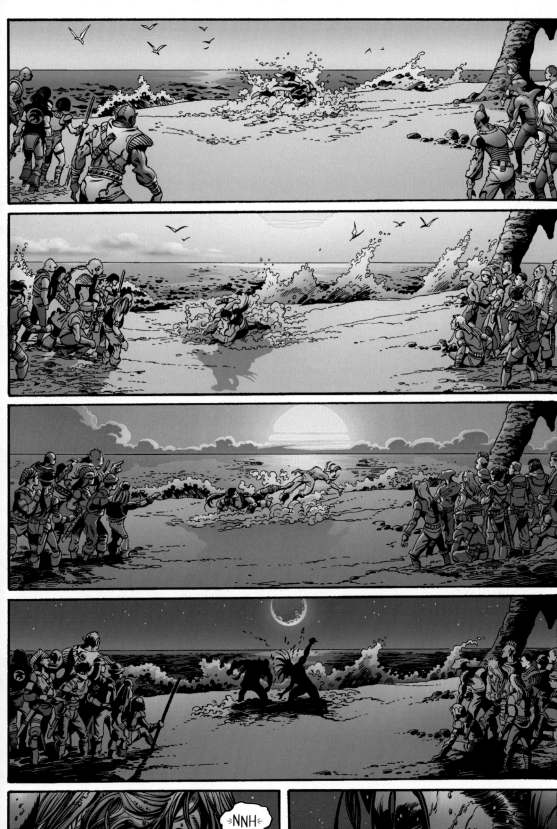

SKAASH

OUR ANCESTOR WAS A FOOL.

ALEXI FORGED THE PEACE WITH THE HERONS, INITIATED THE RITUAL COMBAT TO TAKE THE WAR'S PLACE, BUILT THE ARENA ON THE TOURNAMENT ISLE.

AND WE PRESERVE HIS BLADE LIKE AN HONORED TROPHY.

IS THAT WHAT YOU BELIEVE, MY SON?

WE'D HAVE WIPED THE HERONS FROM THE FACE OF AVALON *LONG AGO* IF NOT FOR ALEXI'S WEAKNESS!

PERHAPS WHAT YOU DEEM WEAKNESS WAS NECESSITY. A WAY TO PRESERVE A KINGDOM WHOSE RESOURCES HAD BEEN EXHAUSTED BY DECADE UPON DECADE OF WAR.

WHILE THE TRUCE HELD, OUR KINGDOM TENDED ITS WOUNDS. WE GREW STRONG. AND NOW WE MAKE WAR AGAIN.

IS IT TRULY EDVIN'S PEACE THAT VEXES YOU, BRON? OR IS IT PERHAPS THE *SCAR* YOU BEAR?

THE WESTERN WHELP WILL PAY FOR HIS TREACHERY! I'LL PUT THIS BLADE TO ITS *PROPER* USE, FATHER, AND OPEN ETHAN'S THROAT AS I DID HIS BROTHER'S!

BRON, YOU ARE MY ELDEST. YOU ARE TO FOLLOW ME TO THE THRONE ONE DAY...

...IF YOU LEARN TO CONTROL YOURSELF. IF YOU MEAN TO BE KING, YOU MUST BE MASTER OF YOUR ANGER, NOT LET IT MASTER YOU.

YOUR TEMPER DOES NOT BEFIT ONE OF RAVEN NOBLE BLOOD. AND IT WILL NOT SIT WELL ON THE HEAD THAT WEARS THE CROWN.

I ADVISE YOU TO THINK ON THESE THINGS, MY SON.

HAVE A SERVANT REMOVE THE MESS YOU MADE...

...BUT KNOW THERE WON'T ALWAYS BE SOMEONE TO CLEAN UP AFTER YOU.

YES, FATHER.

KEEP LOOKING DOWN YOUR NOSE AT ME, OLD MAN...

...YOU'LL NEVER SEE ME BEHIND YOU.

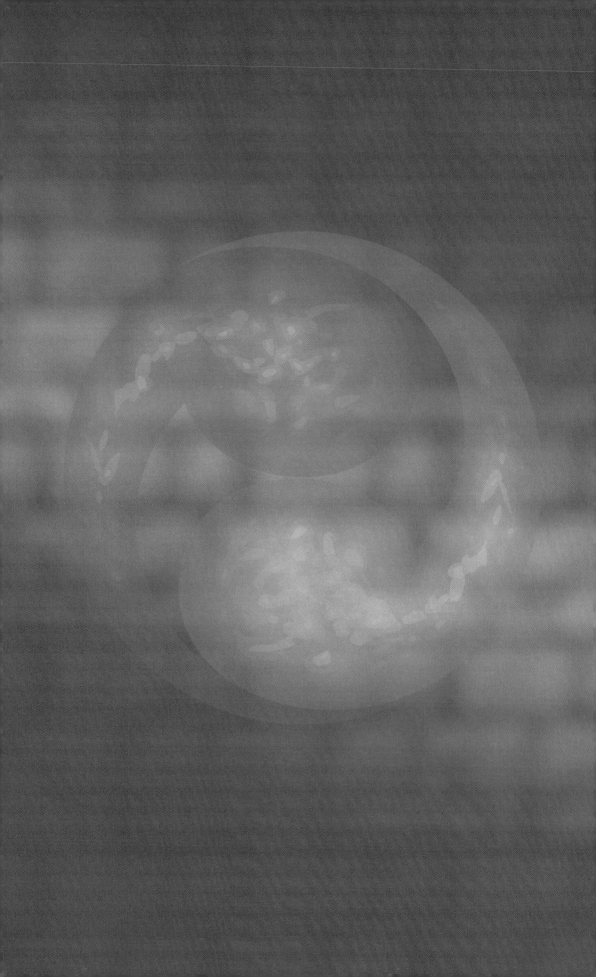

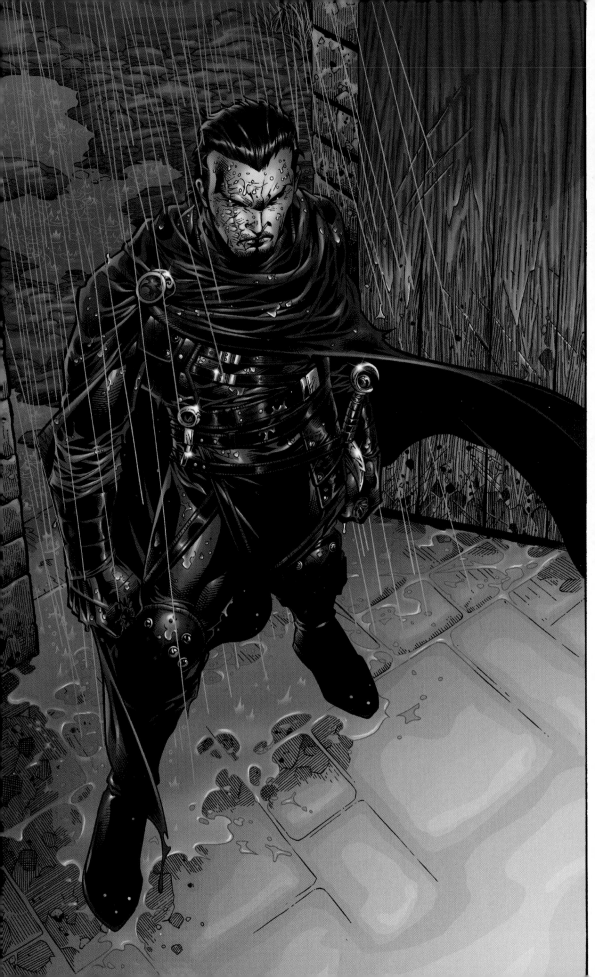

CHAPTER 2

FILTH.

EASY, WASN'T IT?

BUT THEN YOU NEVER FOUND *MURDER* TERRIBLY DIFFICULT ANYWAY.

"WE'RE AT WAR FOR THE FIRST TIME IN TWO CENTURIES, WE GET ROUTED AND DRIVEN FROM THE ENEMY'S SHORES..."

...AND YOU TWO CAN'T FIND ANYTHING BETTER TO DO THAN RIDE OFF AFTER AN ESCAPED SLAVE!

I EXPECT SOMETHING LIKE THIS FROM YOU, BRON, BUT I THOUGHT YOU KNEW BETTER, KORT. IT'S TIME YOU STOPPED BEING SWEPT UP BY YOUR BROTHER'S FITS OF TEMPER.

BY OUR *ANCESTORS*, BRON, YOU'RE NEXT IN LINE FOR THE THRONE. THIS BEHAVIOR ONLY EXACERBATES MY CONCERNS OVER YOUR READINESS TO SUCCEED ME ONE DAY.

NOW THAT YOUR LITTLE ADVENTURE'S CONCLUDED, DID ANYTHING USEFUL COME OF IT?

NO, FATHER...

...NOTHING.

NO, OF COURSE NOT.

I WANT YOU BOTH TO MEET SOMEONE WHO ARRIVED WHILE YOU WERE GONE ON YOUR FOOL'S ERRAND. SOMEONE WHO'S GOING TO BE QUITE USEFUL TO US.

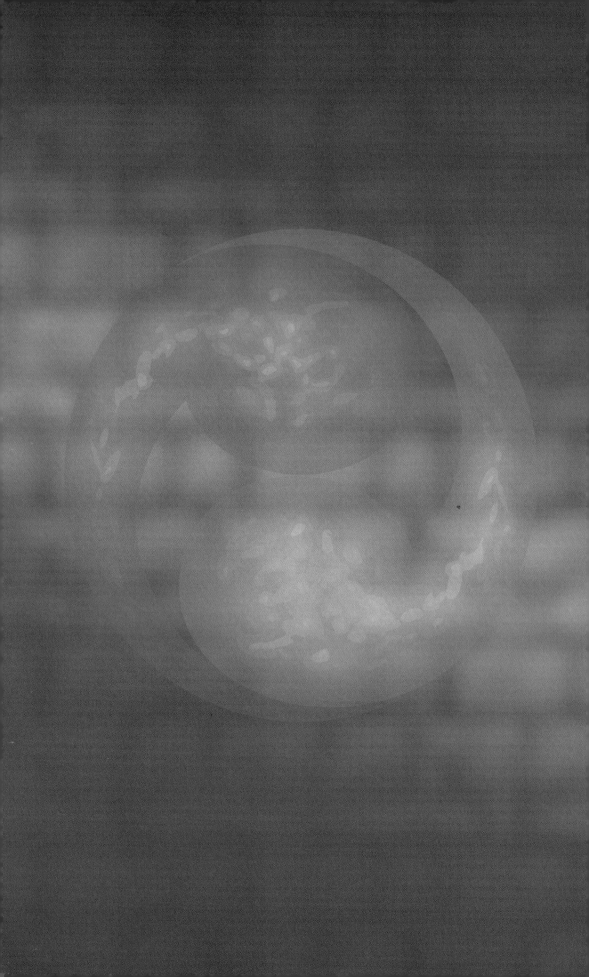

CHAPTER 3

IT'S A PRETTY SMALL VILLAGE, BUT WE SHOULD BE ABLE TO FIND WHAT WE NEED AND GET OUT AGAIN WITHOUT BEING CAUGHT.

THEN WE'LL SEE IF WE CAN FIND ASHLEIGH.

IF YOU STILL THINK SEARCHING FOR ASHLEIGH IS THE BEST COURSE OF ACTION.

SKINK, THE ONE PLACE I KNOW I CAN CONFRONT BRON IS THE RAVEN KEEP. WHEN ASHLEIGH FREED US FROM THE KEEP SHE SAID SHE HAD FRIENDS THERE.

IF THOSE FRIENDS CAN HELP ME GET INTO THE KEEP, I'LL SLAY BRON IN HIS OWN HOME.

AND THAT'S THE ONLY REASON YOU WANT TO FIND ASHLEIGH?

THE ONLY REASON.

LOOKS LIKE THE RAVEN MILITARY IS ALREADY STARTING TO CONSCRIPT TROOPS. LET'S AVOID—

ETHAN! THERE AT THE BACK OF THE DAIS...

YOU'RE RIGHT. LET'S JUST GET THIS OVER WITH.

WHILE THE REST OF THE TOWN IS GAWKING AT THE SOLDIERS WE CAN GET WHAT WE CAME FOR.

THERE'S THE STABLE.

I DIDN'T LIKE STEALING THAT BOAT LAST TIME WE WERE IN THE EAST. I'M NOT ENTIRELY COMFORTABLE WITH *THIS*, EITHER.

THERE'S NOT REALLY ANOTHER CHOICE, ETHAN, IS THERE? IF WE'RE GOING TO COVER ANY GROUND, WE NEED MOUNTS.

I KNOW...

...BUT MY PARENTS DIDN'T RAISE ME TO BE A THIEF. I LEARNED MY LESSON WHEN MY FATHER CAUGHT ME FILCHING PASTRIES FROM THE SERVANTS' LARDER.

DO YOU REMEMBER *THAT?* I WAS SCRUBBING KITCHEN POTS FOR A MONTH.

BDEEP

I JUST WANT TO DO THIS AS QUICKLY AS POSSIBLE AND GET...

...OUT OF HERE.

ETHAN!

WHERE ARE WE HEADED?!

WE FOLLOW THE MAP, SKINK...

...NORTH!

THIS IS THE PLACE...

...BUT THERE'S NOTHING HERE. TWO DAYS' RIDE AND NOTHING BUT RUINS.

NO SIGN OF ASHLEIGH, NO SIGN OF THE UNDERGROUND.

SINCE WE'RE *HERE*, I MIGHT AS WELL HAVE A LOOK AROUND.

BE CAREFUL, ETHAN. SOMETHING FEELS...WRONG... ABOUT THIS PLACE.

ALL MAY NOT BE AS IT APPEARS.

I WONDER WHAT THESE RUINS *WERE*, OUT IN THE MIDDLE OF NOWHERE LIKE THIS.

A BETTER VANTAGE POINT COULDN'T HURT...

...THOUGH I DOUBT THERE'S ANYTHING TO SEE.

NOTHING AT ALL. JUST CRUMBLING BUILDINGS AND A STAIRCASE LEADING NOWHERE.

MAYBE THERE NEVER *WAS* ANYTHING MORE, AND ASHLEIGH WAS JUST—

UHH?

WHAT WAS *THAT?*

SOME KIND OF—

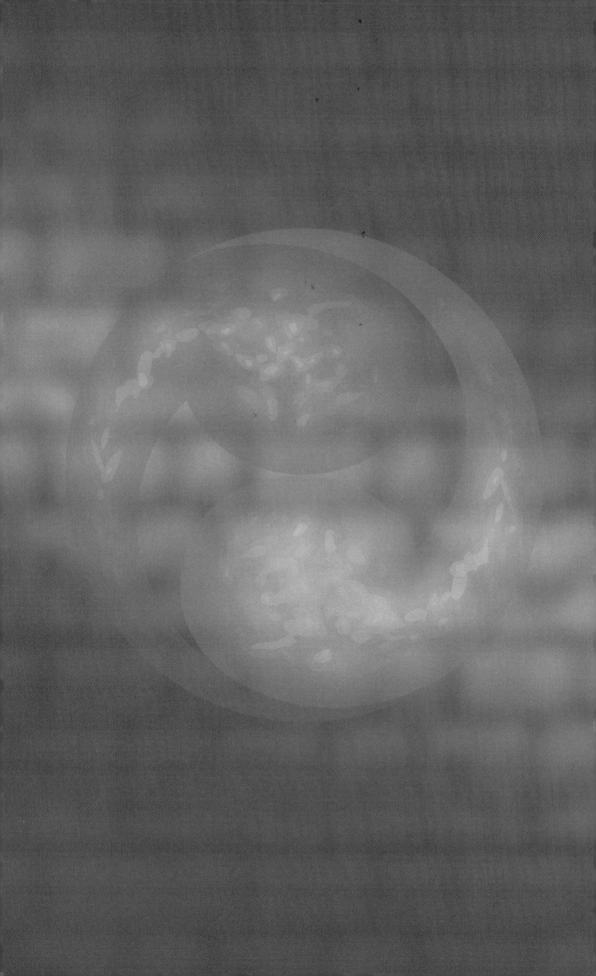

CHAPTER 4

ETHAN!

WHAT *IS* THIS PLACE?

SKINK...

...DON'T DO ANYTHING SUDDEN.

...BECAUSE IF EITHER OF YOU *MOVE* YOU WON'T LIVE LONG ENOUGH TO REGRET IT.

I'M NOT LOOKING FOR TROUBLE.

AND I DON'T MEAN ANY HARM TO THE UNDERGROUND.

ASHLEIGH?

SHE GAVE ME *THIS*...

...AND TOLD ME IT WOULD LEAD ME TO HER.

IF ASHLEIGH TRUSTS YOU ENOUGH TO SEND YOU HERE, THEN YOU'RE WELCOME AMONG US.

APOLOGIES FOR THE HARSH RECEPTION...

...BUT WE CAN'T BE TOO CAREFUL.

Oh.

SORRY, IT'S...

...THE SWORD'S A LONG STORY.

I'M STILL NOT ENTIRELY SURE ABOUT IT.

I'VE TAKEN THE FREE NAME FLITCH. YOU'RE WHO YOU *APPEAR* TO BE?

DEPENDS ON WHO YOU THINK I AM. MY NAME IS ETHAN.

AND THIS IS MY... ...uh... ...*FRIEND*, SKINK.

HOW IS THIS PLACE HIDDEN? I *STUMBLED* INTO IT. LITERALLY.

HOLOGRAM GENERATORS.

WHAT YOU SEE OUT THERE IS ALL THAT'S LEFT OF THE FIRST FREE CITY FOR LESSER RACES IN RAVEN LANDS. THE RUINS ARE REMOTE ENOUGH THAT NO ONE EVER PASSES THROUGH...

...BUT WE SCREEN ANY SIGN THE SANCTUARY EXISTS. COME WITH ME, I'LL SHOW YOU THE REST.

YOU NEED NOT BE A SERVANT, LITTLE BROTHER.

WE'RE FREE HERE, *ALL* OF US.

I'M NOT SURE WHAT YOU WERE EXPECTING...

"...COMPARED TO THE SLAVERY THEY'VE LIVED WITH SINCE BIRTH.

"THE UNDERGROUND INTENDS TO WIN FREEDOM FOR ALL LESSER RACES BY WHATEVER MEANS NECESSARY. THE SANCTUARY'S A *START*..."

...IT PROVES SUCH A THING IS POSSIBLE.

ETHAN, THERE'S SOMEONE YOU SHOULD MEET.

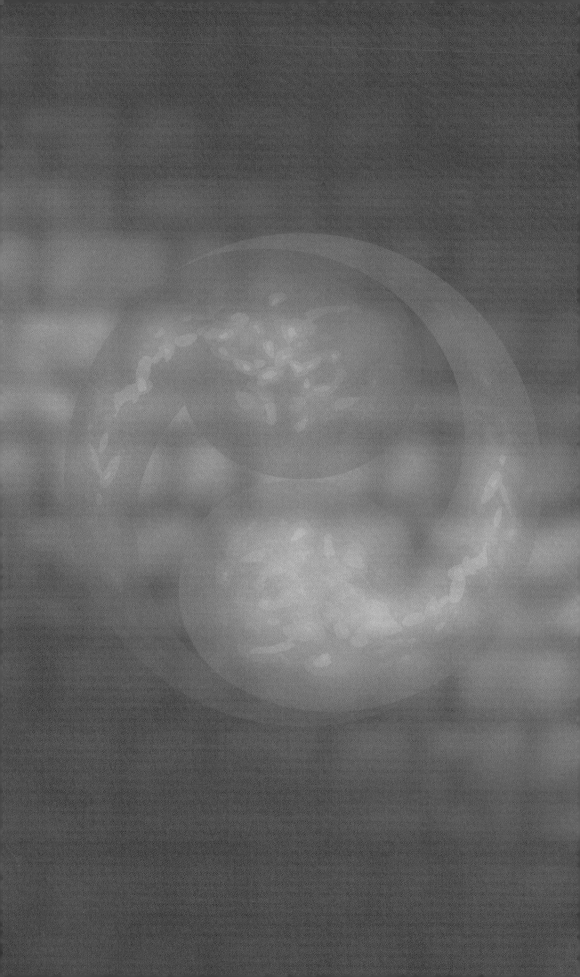

CHAPTER 5

YOU ACT AS IF THE BATTLE WAS DEVOID OF ACHIEVEMENT. I *SLEW* ONE OF THEIR PRINCES.

AND IT SERVED ONLY TO STIFFEN THE HERON RESOLVE. YOU COULD HAVE MADE A PRISONER OF HIM...

...BUT INSTEAD YOU CHOSE TO MAKE A MARTYR OF YOUR ENEMY.

I SALVAGED WHAT I COULD AND ESCAPED WITH ENOUGH OF OUR ARMY INTACT TO FIGHT ANOTHER DAY!

IS *ANYTHING* EVER GOOD ENOUGH FOR YOU?

ANYTHING?

I WON'T TOLERATE THESE OUTBURSTS IN MY WAR ROOM.

LEAVE.

AS YOU WISH.

BUT I SWEAR TO YOU, FATHER...

...THE DAY WILL COME WHEN YOU WON'T BE ABLE TO DISMISS ME SO EASILY.

FATHER?

I CHECKED THE WAR ROOM, BUT THEY TOLD ME YOU'D ALREADY LEFT.

I THOUGHT THIS MIGHT BE THE BEST PLACE TO LOOK.

YOU KNOW ME TOO WELL, DAUGHTER.

THERE WAS NOTHING MORE TO BE ACCOMPLISHED BY STARING AT THE SAME MAP TABLES AND CALCULATING TROOP STRENGTHS YET AGAIN.

THE HERONS HAVE LANDED AND TAKEN A COASTAL GARRISON, THE ONE I'D PLACED UNDER KORT'S COMMAND.

THANKFULLY HE WAS ABLE TO AVOID CAPTURE.

OR A WORSE FATE.

I COME TO THE THRONE HALL HOPING TO DRAW INSPIRATION FROM THOSE WHO GUIDED OUR DYNASTY IN THE PAST.

PARTICULARLY WHEN IT'S OUR DYNASTY'S *FUTURE* THAT CONCERNS ME.

BECAUSE OF THE WAR?

NO.

NOT THE WAR.

WALK WITH ME.

I WAS STILL A YOUNG MAN WHEN I INHERITED THE THRONE FROM MY MOTHER. NOW MY BONES CREAK WHEN I GET OUT OF BED EACH MORNING.

I'M OLD, ASHLEIGH. NO ONE RULES FOREVER.

BRON IS THE ELDEST. HE'S TO FOLLOW ME TO THAT THRONE...

...AND HE'S NOT READY. I HAVE GRAVE DOUBTS HE EVER *WILL* BE.

THE MANTLE OF RULERSHIP DOES NOT REST EASILY ON THOSE OF HIS TEMPERAMENT.

HE'S TOO QUICK TO ANGER, TOO PRONE TO CASUAL VIOLENCE.

PERHAPS HIS NATURE IS THE PRODUCT OF HIS MOTHER NOT BEING ALIVE TO RAISE HIM. I DON'T KNOW.

GENERATIONS OF OUR FAMILY HAVE TAKEN THEIR PLACE ON THE RAVEN THRONE. SOME BETTER, SOME WORSE, BUT THE *DYNASTY* HAS ALWAYS SURVIVED.

PLEASE, *SIT*.

WHAT?

FATHER, IT'S NOT MY PLACE TO SIT UPON THE THRONE.

I WISH IT *WERE*.

IT WOULD BE...

...SAVE FOR THE SIMPLE TIMING OF YOUR BIRTH. IF ONLY YOU'D BEEN BORN FIRST, *YOU* WOULD BE IN LINE TO RULE.

THERE'S NOTHING TO BE DONE ABOUT IT, FATHER.

WHATEVER HIS FAULTS, IT'S BRON'S BIRTHRIGHT.

TRADITION DEMANDS THE ELDEST ASCENDS TO THE THRONE.

PERHAPS IT'S TIME TRADITION IS BROKEN.

YOU'RE NOT SERIOUSLY CONSIDERING SUCH A THING?

I MIGHT...

...IF I KNEW MY CHOSEN SUCCESSOR WOULD PLACE NO *OTHER* CAUSES BEFORE THOSE OF HER BLOODLINE.

OTHER CAUSES? I'M NOT SURE WHAT—

DON'T INSULT ME. DO YOU THINK I RULE AN ENTIRE KINGDOM BUT REMAIN IGNORANT OF MY OWN FAMILY'S WORKINGS?

BRON *DID* TELL YOU.

BRON TOLD ME *NOTHING.*

I'VE BEEN AWARE OF YOUR INVOLVEMENT WITH THE UNDERGROUND FOR SOME TIME. THE CLUES WERE PLAIN ENOUGH.

BUT AS LONG AS YOU DIDN'T CREATE UNDUE STRIFE WITHIN THE KINGDOM...

...I LOOKED THE OTHER WAY.

TRUE PASSION FOR A CAUSE IS AN ADMIRABLE QUALITY, ASHLEIGH. BUT YOUR PASSION IS MISPLACED.

IT'S TIME YOU PUT ASIDE THE THINGS OF YOUR WILD YOUTH AND TOOK YOUR PLACE WITH YOUR FAMILY.

IT'S POSSIBLE SOME ACCOMMODATION EVENTUALLY CAN BE MADE FOR THE UNDERGROUND AND LESSER RACES.

BUT NOW YOUR LOYALTY MUST BE *HERE.*

I MUST HAVE YOUR SUPPORT IN WHAT'S AHEAD. I'VE INDULGED YOUR INDISCRETIONS AND ASKED LITTLE OF YOU IN RETURN.

NOW I ASK YOU TO PLACE YOUR DYNASTY AND YOUR KINGDOM FIRST.

WILL YOU GIVE ME YOUR LOYALTY WHEN I NEED IT?

BUT...

...BUT, FATHER, I'M...

...YES.

WHAT DID YOU DO TO ME?
GAVE YOU A SMALL PART OF WHAT I AM.
AND WHAT CAN I DO?
ANYTHING...
...ANYTHING AT ALL.

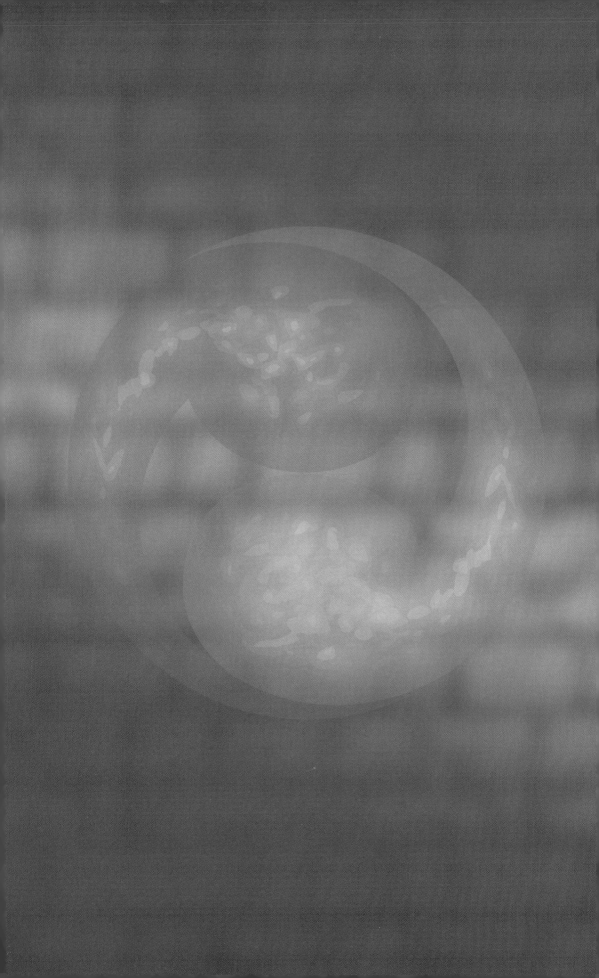

CHAPTER 6

...OUR *DYNASTY'S* FUTURE. I GROW CONCERNED FOR THIS KINGDOM OUR FAMILY HAS BUILT. I WANT TO BE CERTAIN ALL WE HAVE ACHIEVED WILL *CONTINUE* WHEN I AM NO MORE.

I'M SURE THESE ARE THOUGHTS *YOU* SHARE, BRON.

THE WEIGHT OF HISTORY IS A HEAVY THING, FATHER.

WE TRACE OUR LINEAGE IN A DIRECT LINE, AN UNBROKEN SUCCESSION FROM PARENT TO ELDEST CHILD DATING BACK CENTURIES.

IT'S *ALWAYS* BEEN SO.

I HAVE KNOWN FROM THE TIME I WAS A CHILD THAT THE RESPONSIBILITY FOR THE THRONE, FOR THE FUTURE OF THE RAVEN DYNASTY, WOULD BE MINE.

IT IS MY *BIRTHRIGHT.*

I HELD THAT KNOWLEDGE CLOSE AND PREPARED MYSELF FOR IT EVERY DAY OF MY LIFE.

AND YET YOU WOULD PLACE *ASHLEIGH* ON THE THRONE RATHER THAN ME.

SO.

THE WALLS TRULY DO HAVE EARS.

WHY WOULD YOU DO THIS TO ME, FATHER?

BECAUSE THE RESPONSIBILITY OF TRUE POWER IS FAR DIFFERENT THAN THE SIMPLE EXERCISE OF AUTHORITY.

THE THRONE BELONGS TO THE FIRST BORN.

I *WILL* CLAIM IT.

YOU CAN'T MANAGE TO CONTROL *YOURSELF*...

...HOW DO YOU THINK YOU COULD EVER CONTROL AN ENTIRE EMPIRE?

YOU'RE NO MORE PREPARED TO LEAD THIS KINGDOM THAN IS THAT DAMN HOUND OF YOURS.

AND YOU GIVE ME NO SIGN YOU EVER *WILL* BE.

CRUELTY FOR ITS OWN SAKE AND FITS OF TEMPER DON'T BEFIT A MONARCH.

IF TRADITION DEMANDS I PLACE MY KINGDOM IN THE HANDS OF A PETULANT CHILD, THEN TRADITION BE DAMNED.

I WON'T ALLOW THE MERE TIMING OF YOUR SISTER'S BIRTH TO PREVENT THE FITTEST RULER FROM FOLLOWING ME TO THE RAVEN THRONE.

I'M SORRY, FATHER...

FATHER? I REALIZE IT'S LATE, BUT...

WHEN WILL I BE ABLE TO DO THAT?

YOU ALREADY *CAN*. THAT AND *MORE*.

I'VE *GIVEN* YOU THE POWER, ALL YOU NEED DO IS LEARN TO HARNESS IT.

AND I'M A *VERY* GOOD TEACHER.

I ALWAYS INTENDED TO SHIFT THE BLAME TO ASHLEIGH. HER WALKING IN MADE IT THAT MUCH EASIER.

I'LL SUMMON THE GUARDS AND HAVE HER TAKEN TO THE DUNGEONS.

WHAT OF YOUR BROTHER?

WILL HE PRESENT ANY DIFFICULTIES?

KORT'S NEVER BEEN TERRIBLY CLEVER. HE'LL BELIEVE WHATEVER I TELL HIM.

HE'S ALWAYS BEEN TERRIFIED SOMETHING WOULD HAPPEN TO ME. HE'S NEVER WANTED THE THRONE HIMSELF.

KORT WILL BE A BOON IN ALL THIS.

SEND HIM HERE BUT TELL HIM NOTHING. I WANT HIM TO HEAR OF HIS SISTER'S TREACHERY FROM HIS DEAR BROTHER'S LIPS. NO...

...IN FACT, SEND HIM TO THE THRONE ROOM.

WHERE *ELSE* WOULD THE KING BE?

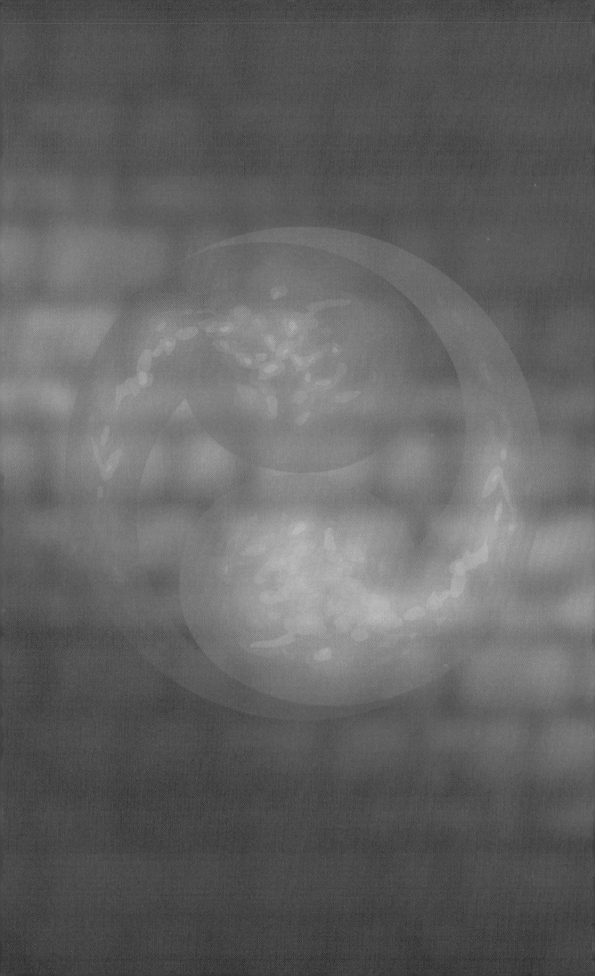

CHAPTER 7

YOUR BROTHER CUT *MY* BROTHER'S THROAT!

ALL THIS TIME, AND YOU DIDN'T SAY *ANYTHING*.

WHAT DID YOU *WANT* ME TO DO? HANG A SIGN AROUND MY NECK?

I SHOULD HAVE KNOWN.

THE WAY YOU GOT IN AND OUT OF THE KEEP, SEEING YOU ON THE BATTLEFIELD, THE REACTION TO YOUR NAME AT THE SANCTUARY.

EVEN THE *DOG*.

IT ALL MAKES SENSE...

...BECAUSE YOU'RE *ONE* OF THEM.

YOU SAY *"ONE OF THEM"* LIKE IT'S A CRIME.

YOU WANT ME TO BE ASHAMED OF BEING PART OF THE RAVEN DYNASTY? I'M *NOT*.

YOU DIDN'T KNOW WHO I WAS BECAUSE I'M THE YOUNGEST CHILD. WE'RE *TRADITIONALLY* KEPT OUT OF THE PUBLIC EYE.

BUT MY HERITAGE DOESN'T CHANGE MY LOYALTY TO THE UNDERGROUND. IT DOESN'T CHANGE WHO I *AM*.

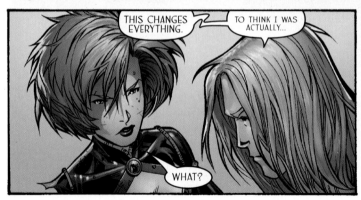

THIS CHANGES EVERYTHING.

TO THINK I WAS ACTUALLY...

WHAT?

NOTHING.

SO YOU DELIVER YOURSELF TO ME, ETHAN.

I DON'T KNOW WHETHER TO BE IMPRESSED YOU MADE IT THIS FAR, OR AMUSED THAT YOU'RE FOOLHARDY ENOUGH TO CHALLENGE ME AT THE VERY HEART OF MY POWER.

KILLING MY BROTHER WASN'T ENOUGH FOR YOU, BUTCHER?

YOU HAD TO MURDER YOUR OWN *FATHER* AS WELL?

MY FATHER?

I'M AFRAID YOU'RE MISINFORMED. THE TRUTH, AS TERRIBLE AS IT MAY BE, IS THAT MY *SISTER* WAS RESPONSIBLE FOR THE KING'S DEATH.

SO TRAGIC WHEN A SIBLING GOES BAD...

...THOUGH I SUPPOSE IN YOUR CASE YOU HAVE *ONE LESS* TO WORRY ABOUT.

ALMOST AS TRAGIC AS THE DEATH OF AN HEIR TO THE THRONE.

YES, WELL...

...*I'M* HEIR NO LONGER.

THE THRONE AND ALL ITS RESPONSIBILITIES HAVE PASSED TO ME.

FITTING, DON'T YOU THINK, FOR ME TO START MY REIGN BY KILLING *YOU?*

THAT'S IRONIC.

I THOUGHT I'D *END* YOUR REIGN BY KILLING *YOU.*

TRY.

CHAPTER 8

DIED? *HOW*? WHAT'S HAPPENED?

THE DETAILS AREN'T COMPLETELY CLEAR, BUT WE KNOW THE KING IS DEAD.

THE YOUNGEST CHILD IS RUMORED RESPONSIBLE.

REGICIDE.

VIKTOR FORCED THIS WAR, BUT I WOULD NOT HAVE WISHED THIS FATE UPON HIM.

THE THRONE BELONGS TO THE ELDEST NOW? TO *BRON*?

AYE, FATHER.

THE MAN WHO *MURDERED* ARTOR NOW SITS UPON THE RAVEN THRONE.

THIS BODES ILL FOR THE WAR.

HOW SO? WON'T THIS THROW THE RAVENS INTO A DISARRAY THAT WILL BE TO OUR ADVANTAGE?

I *KNEW* VIKTOR. I COULD PREDICT HIM.

AT *BEST* BRON IS A WILD CARD. AT WORST HE COULD BE A MADMAN.

AND ETHAN WENT TO THE EAST VOWING TO SLAY HIM.

IT GIVES ME NO COMFORT KNOWING *YLENA* IS IN THE EAST AS WELL, BUT AT LEAST SHE'S SECURE BEHIND THE WALLS OF THE FORTRESS SHE AND HER TROOPS TOOK.

WITH ETHAN...

...WE HAVE NO WAY OF KNOWING IF HE'S EVEN *ALIVE*.

I WANT THIS PIECE OF MEAT REMOVED FROM MY THRONE HALL...

...AND HAVE THAT HUMPBACKED FREAK EXECUTED AS WELL.

COME ALONG.

I WON'T LET THIS END LIKE—

YOU WEREN'T SATISFIED WITH FATHER...

RUDD!

WE NEED YOUR HELP.

ASHLEIGH?

I WASN'T *EXPECTING* YOU...

TO WHAT DO I OWE THE SURPRISE?

I DON'T HAVE MUCH TIME TO EXPLAIN, RUDD, BUT BRON'S MURDERED MY FATHER AND TAKEN THE THRONE.

HE'S BLAMING *ME* FOR THE CRIME. HE WOULD'VE HAD ME EXECUTED IF I HADN'T ESCAPED.

I KNOW YOUR BROTHER'S A BAD SEED, BUT *THIS*...

I DAMN *MYSELF* FOR NOT SEEING IT IN TIME.

RUDD, WE NEED TO BE OUT OF THE CITY AND ON OUR WAY TO THE SANCTUARY.

YOUR FRIEND CAN BE TRUSTED?

HE'S EVEN MORE OF A FUGITIVE THAN I AM.

ETHAN, THIS IS RUDD. THE UNDERGROUND HAS SUPPORTERS *OTHER* THAN ME.

THAT'S A *RECOGNIZABLE* FACE YOU WEAR, PRINCE.

YOU'RE LUCKY YOU FELL IN WITH ASHLEIGH.

DEET

WHERE DOES IT LEAD?

IT'LL TAKE YOU OUT TO THE BARRENS BEYOND THE CITY WALLS.

WHRRRRRRRRR

MORE THAN A FEW LESSER RACE SLAVES HAVE USED IT TO LEAVE THEIR CHAINS BEHIND.

THERE ARE LANTERNS AND FOOD WAITING DOWN THERE.

THANK YOU, RUDD.

ANYTHING FOR YOU, ASHLEIGH. YOU KNOW THAT.

GET YOURSELVES MOVING RIGHT AWAY. AND BE CAREFUL. YOUR BROTHER'S GOING TO TEAR APART THIS CITY LOOKING FOR YOU.

YOU BE CAREFUL, TOO. BRON'S HANDS DON'T NEED ANY MORE BLOOD ON THEM.

IT'S NOT MY BLOOD HE WANTS.

THANK YOU. FOR HELPING US.

YOU THANK ME BY TAKING CARE OF ASHLEIGH.

This contemplative Ashleigh is by CrossGen penciler Andrea Di Vito who was aided and abetted by inker John Dell and colorist Caesar Rodriguez.

RONICLES 2
Ron Marz
George Pérez
Dennis Jensen & Rick Magyar
Laura DePuy

ION 8-10
Ron Marz
Jim Cheung
Don Hillsman II
Caesar Rodriguez

ION 11
Ron Marz
Jim Cheung
Don Hillsman II
Justin Ponsor

ION 12
Ron Marz
Andrea Di Vito
Rob Hunter
Paul Mounts

ION 13-14
Ron Marz
Jim Cheung
Don Hillsman II
Justin Ponsor

LETTERERS
Dave Lanphear
Troy Peteri

The CrossGen Universe created by Mark Alessi & Gina M. Villa

Mark Alessi
Publisher & CEO

Gina M. Villa
Chief Operating Officer

Michael A. Beattie
Chief Financial Officer

Tony Panaccio
VP Product Development

Chris Oarr
Director of Marketing & Sales

James Breitbeil
Director of Marketing & Distribution

Ian M. Feller
Director of Corporate Communications

Courtland Whited
MIS Director

Michael Creed
Network Administrator

Barbara Kesel
Head Writer

Bart Sears
Art Director

Pam Davies
Production Director

Sylvia Bretz
Janet Bechtle
Production Assistants

Michelle Pugliese
Freelance Coordinator

Michael Atiyeh
Karla Barnett
Tony Bedard
Amber Boonyaratapalin
Andrew Crossley
Frank D'Armata
Charles Decker
John Dell
Steve Epting
Fabrizio Fiorentino
Drew Geraci
Butch Guice
Morry Hollowell
Tammy Jackson
Jeff Johnson
Jason Lambert
Greg Land
Ron Marz
Steve McNiven
David Meikis
Karl Moline
Tiffany Moncada
Paul Pelletier
Mark Pennington
Brandon Peterson
James Rochelle
Matt Ryan
Rob Schwager
Tom Simmons
Andy Smith
John Smith
Beth Widera